Look out for other Little Tim titles by
Edward Ardizzone published by Scholastic:

TIM IN DANGER

by
Edward Ardizzone

SCHOLASTIC
PRESS

For my nephew, Simon

Scholastic Children's Books,
Commonwealth House, 1-19 New Oxford Street,
London WC1A 1NU, UK
A division of Scholastic Ltd
London ~ New York ~ Toronto ~ Sydney ~ Auckland
Mexico City ~ New Delhi ~ Hong Kong

First published by Oxford University Press, 1953
This edition published by Scholastic Ltd, 2000

ISBN 0 439 01040 3 (HB)
ISBN 0 439 01041 1 (PB)

Origination by Colourpath Ltd, London
Printed by Proost, Belgium

It was a lovely day when Tim, Charlotte
and Ginger were playing on the beach. The
sky was blue, the sea was blue, and the
white yachts were sailing in the bay.

But something was wrong with Ginger. He would mope.

Charlotte thought that he was remembering the time when he was a ship's boy and was pining for a life at sea once more. She was right, for early the next morning, when Tim woke up, he found Ginger's bed empty and a note from Ginger on it to say that he had run away.

Tim quickly called Charlotte and they decided to go and find him at once.

First they hurriedly got dressed, then Tim wrote a note for his mother to tell her not to worry and that they would be back soon.

When this was done they both set off to the station to take the train to the seaport town.

As they were walking along they met their friend the market gardener who was taking his vegetables to the town. He was a kind man and gave them a lift in his van all the way, so they saved their train fares.

Once at the town they went straight to the docks and there they asked everybody they met if they had seen Ginger.

But nobody had.

After a time they became tired with wandering about and asking questions, and feeling rather sad they sat down on a bollard to rest.

As they were sitting there they had a
great surprise. They were watching a small
steamer sail slowly out of the dock, when
at one of the portholes a face appeared

crowned with a mop of red hair. Charlotte immediately recognized it as Ginger's.

"Oh dear," said Tim, "we can't follow him now. We must go home without him."

You can imagine how sad they were, but worse was to follow. When Tim felt in his pocket for the money to buy their railway tickets home, it had gone.
There must have been a hole in his pocket.

Oh! What shall we do

It was getting dark now and beginning to rain. Charlotte, who was tired and hungry, began to cry. Tim was tired and hungry too.

They crept into
a warehouse to
shelter from the rain.
There they found a
corner among some
packing cases in
which to rest. Soon
they were asleep.

But they had not been asleep for long when
they were roughly
woken by a man's
voice saying,
"WHAT ARE
YOU DOING
HERE?"

Bleimey! Whal's this coming aboard?

Tim told the man their story and how they had no money to go home with.

"Hm!" said the man. "You can't stay here. Can you work?"

Tim said "Yes, I have been a ship's boy before and Charlotte can cook and sew."

"Very well," said the man. "I am the captain of a ship. We sail almost at once. I am short of crew so will sign you on. Mr Bosun, take them aboard and make them work."

Soon after this the ship sailed. Tim and Charlotte had a chance to slip on deck and watch as the ship steamed out of the harbour in the evening light.

Though it was now dark it was a long time before Tim or Charlotte could go to bed. Tired as she was, Charlotte had to peel lots of potatoes, while Tim was given a bucket of water and a brush and made to clean out the seamen's quarters.

Tim was tired too, but he was also unhappy about his parents. They would be so upset when he and Charlotte did not come home. How could he let them know?

Luckily he met an officer who seemed friendly and who promised to ask the wireless operator to send a message. This made Tim feel much happier.

For the first few days Charlotte found the work very hard and when she was alone in her bunk she could not help crying a little and wishing she was at home. But, as she was a very good cook, she soon became a great favourite with the crew.

I say, that smells good

Tim found the work hard too and was often very bored with scrubbing and cleaning. However, as he always tried to do his best and never complained, everybody was very nice to him.

Tim and Charlotte's best friend on board was the second mate. He was a very fat man and a very sad one too. He was sad because he was always unlucky and felt that nobody liked him. He was, however, a kind man and would often say "Now children, stop work and sit down and talk to me."

Then they would tell him about their home by the sea and about Tim's mother and father and Ginger. He would sigh and say that he wished he had a nice home like other people.

To tell you the truth he was really very unlucky. Everything he did went wrong.

The captain would get terribly cross with him and the sailors would tease him and call him 'Fatty' behind his back. Even the ship's cat, who was friendly with everybody,

would have nothing to do with him.

One day when Charlotte was sitting on the deck darning the sailors' socks, she noticed that the second mate looked sadder than ever. She asked him what the matter was. "Oh dear," he said. "It is my birthday the day after tomorrow, and nobody will

remember it. In any case, I am so unlucky something horrid always happens on my birthday."

Charlotte felt so sorry for him that she decided to make him a birthday cake as a surprise. A very fine cake it was too. It was full of currants and sultanas and had lots of almond icing.

Tim, who was good at drawing, iced it beautifully.

On top of the cake he drew a picture of the ship in blue and red sugar.

That night the weather grew worse. The sea had a cold and oily swell which made the ship rattle and rock; but worse still, there was fog.

The fog crept into the seamen's quarters and made them cough as they lay in their bunks.

It crept into the galley where Tim and Charlotte were reading and writing and made their eyes smart, and the ship's cat sneeze.

It crept into the second mate's cabin and made him more miserable than ever.

It crept on to the bridge and made it difficult for the man at the wheel to keep his course or the lookout man to see ahead.

It worried the officers terribly. They could not see where they were going.

The next morning the fog was worse than ever. The captain and all the officers were on the bridge peering ahead. The ship's foghorn was going 'Moo Moo'. Suddenly there were shouts of "We are going to collide, look out!"

Then there was the sound of bells and reversing engines followed by a terrible crash. After that for a short time there was silence.

They had run straight into another ship and cut it in half. The halves were sinking.

Tim and Charlotte rushed on deck and there they saw a terrible sight. The two halves of the sinking ship could just be seen.

In the water, men were struggling and shouting for help, while life belts were thrown to them and boats lowered to the rescue.

The captain ordered Charlotte to go below to the galley to make tea and prepare bandages, as the rescued men would be very cold and some would be badly hurt.

Tim was ordered to help lower the life boats.

Soon all the sailors that were in the water were saved and the captain had decided to leave the scene of the disaster, when Tim, who had very sharp eyes, noticed a dim red shape that looked like a boy lying on the forepart of the sinking

ship. He pointed it out to the captain who immediately ordered a boat to go to the rescue with the second mate in charge. Tim was in the boat too. He had jumped in without waiting for permission.

When they arrived at the wreck Tim was

the first on
board and he
was astonished
to discover
Ginger lying
unconscious
on the deck.

Now they were all in great danger,
because, at any minute, the wreck might
sink and drag them
down to the
bottom of
the sea.

But in spite of the danger they calmly went about the difficult job of lowering the unconscious Ginger into the boat and they did it only just in time; because no sooner

had they done so and rowed a few yards off than the forepart of the ship plunged beneath the waves.

In the meantime, Charlotte was down below in the seamen's quarters bandaging

the men who had been hurt and giving them hot sweet tea to drink.

You can imagine how surprised she was when Ginger was carried down and laid

at her feet, and how anxious she was too when she saw him unconscious.

However, blankets, hot water bottles and tea soon made him better.

The next day Tim and Charlotte were so busy looking after the wounded men and talking to Ginger, who was now quite well,

that they quite forgot the second mate's birthday, and only remembered it when they saw the cake in the galley.

They decided to take it to him at once. Charlotte carried it and followed by Tim and Ginger they marched to the second mate's cabin. (But, of course, they could not put any candles on the cake because they did not know his age.)

There they found him looking dreadfully sad.

However, he soon cheered up when he saw the cake and insisted on their each having a slice.

Then the captain came in and congratulated him on the brave way he had helped to rescue the ship-wrecked sailors. He congratulated Tim and Charlotte too and said that Charlotte had done splendid work in looking after the wounded men.

After this the weather became fine and calm. The men who had been hurt sat on deck in the sun and soon got well.

Charlotte was busier than ever with the extra sailors to feed, but she had Tim and Ginger to help her.

The second mate was very happy. The sailors obeyed all his orders and never called him 'Fatty'.

And, of course, Tim and Charlotte and Ginger, too, were favourites with everybody.

When they arrived in port Tim sent a telegram to his parents saying "Have found Ginger will be home soon."

Then, with the money he and Charlotte had earned, they bought railway tickets for their journey home.

The second mate and the crew came to see them off at the station.

It was a long journey, but as they had a splendid dinner on the train and had bought lots of books and magazines to read they were not a bit bored.

When they arrived home Tim's mother and father were so pleased to see them that they quite forgot to be cross with Ginger for having run away.

— The End —